Regina's Big Mistake

MARISSA MOSS

ALLSTON BRANCH LIBRARY
Houghton Mifflin Company
Boston

For Harvey

Library of Congress Cataloging-in-Publication Data

Moss, Marissa.
   Regina's big mistake / Marissa Moss.
      p.   cm.
   Summary: When told to draw a jungle in art class, Regina
experiences feelings of failure and creative insecurity, but manages
to create a beautiful picture that's all her own.
   RNF 0-395-55330-X PAP ISBN 0-395-70093-0
   {1. Drawing — Fiction. 2. Artists — Fiction. 3. Self-confidence —
Fiction. 4. Schools — Fiction.}   I. Title.
PZ7.M8535Re   1990   90-32740
{E} — dc20   CIP
                                AC

Printed in the United States of America
WOZ   10 9 8 7 6

Everyone in Mrs. Li's class got a piece of paper.
Everyone was supposed to draw a jungle or a rain forest.
That meant Regina, too.

Regina stared at the big, blank piece of paper in front of her. Her fingers froze on her crayon. Where should she begin?

Stuart had already drawn two trees thick with leaves. Nathalie was concentrating on a fierce lion.

All around Regina jungles sprouted up. But her paper stayed blank.

"What are you making," joked Joshua, "an invisible jungle? Ha!"

Regina blushed. She hunched over her paper and lightly touched it
with the tip of her crayon. She started to draw a jungle flower. She drew one
petal, then another. But the second petal was bigger than the first one.

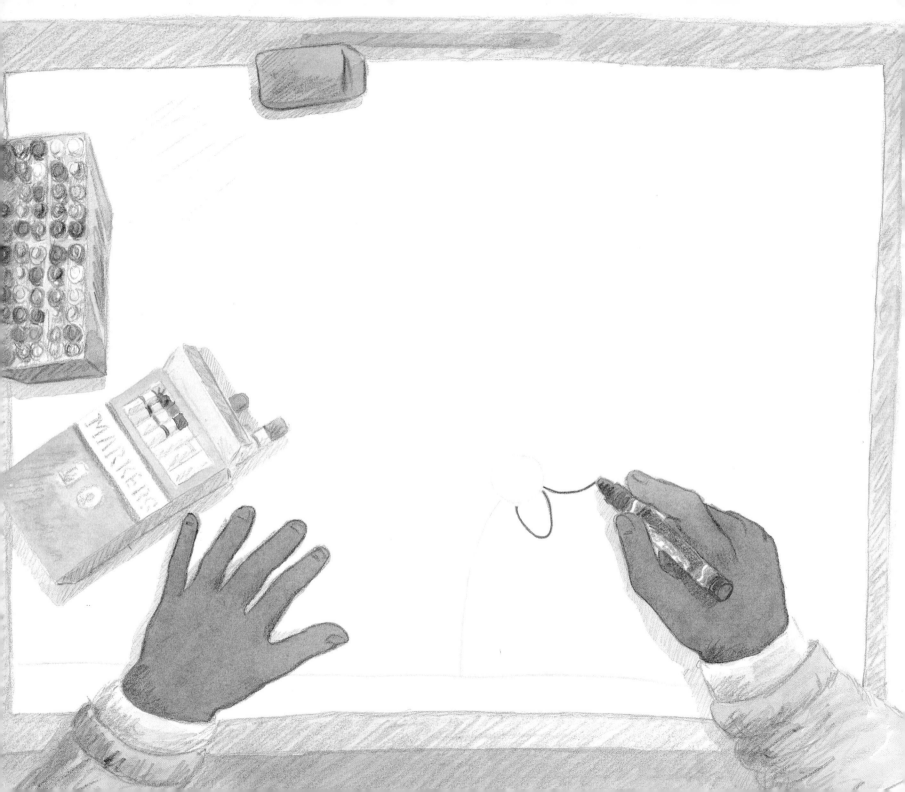

Regina groaned. A mistake! She tried to erase the second petal, but crayon doesn't erase, and she tore the paper instead. She crumpled it up quickly, before anyone could see her ugly mistake.

"What happened to your drawing?" asked Mrs. Li.

"I made a mistake," Regina mumbled.

"Well, try to draw around it next time," said Mrs. Li. "You're wasting paper."

Regina smoothed her new piece of paper.
Anything was possible as long as it was empty. But somehow her hand could never draw what she saw in her head.

Stuart's jungle was almost finished now, full of strange, ripe fruits and colorful birds. Nathalie's lion stalked an antelope. Regina wanted to cry. She could never draw anything so beautiful.

"Almost done?" asked Mrs. Li. "Ten more minutes."

Regina picked up a brown crayon. She had to draw something. Carefully, she started to draw a tree like Stuart's.

"Hey, don't copy me!" he growled.

"I'm not," said Regina, and she quickly drew three big branches on her tree. But those heavy branches made her tree look funny.

Regina bit her lip. Was this another mistake? Could she draw around it, like Mrs. Li said? She looked again at the jungles growing around her.

"It's not a mistake. I can fix it," muttered Regina. She started to draw a lion under the tree.

"Copycat!" said Nathalie with a sneer.

"I am not!" Regina gulped. "My lion is different from yours." And she quickly drew a tongue hanging out of the lion's mouth.

"My lion's thirsty," said Regina. "He needs water." So she drew a lake, then a frog, some fish, and a duck to go in the lake, and some flowers alongside it. The jungle grew and grew until it filled the paper.

Regina smiled. All her jungle needed now was a sun. She carefully drew a yellow circle, but the crayon wobbled and the circle had a dent in it.

"I've ruined it!" she cried. "Just when it was getting good!"

"No more paper," warned Mrs. Li. "You'll have to make the best of it."

"Yeah," joked Joshua, "just pretend it's a very lumpy banana."

Regina looked hard at the wobbly circle. It wasn't a sun. But it wasn't a lumpy banana, either. Suddenly she recognized what it was. It was a moon! She drew a face in her moon and surrounded it with stars and comets and a purple-black sky.

"Wow!" said Stuart. "What a great idea! A jungle at night!"

"I wish I'd thought of that," said Nathalie.

Mrs. Li tacked all the pictures up on the wall.

"Good work, Regina," she said, smiling. "I love your moon."

The jungles glowed with their bright colors.
Each one was different. Each one was beautiful.
And even with all her mistakes, Regina thought
hers was perfect.

Regina